D1474097

Also by Claude Simon
in English

Claude Simon

The Invitation

Translated by Jim Cross
with an Afterword by Lois Oppenheim

Dalkey Archive Press

TRANSLATOR'S ACKNOWLEDGMENTS: *Many thanks to all the excellent professors of the Montclair State French department, and especially Drs. Oppenheim and Wilkins.*

Originally published by Les Éditions de Minuit, 1987
© 1987 by Les Éditions de Minuit

This translation © 1991 by Jim Cross
Afterword © 1991 by Lois Oppenheim

Library of Congress Cataloging-in-Publication Data
Simon, Claude.
    [Invitation. English]
    The invitation / Claude Simon: translated by Jim Cross: afterword by
Lois Oppenheim.
    Translation of: L'invitation.
    1. Soviet Union—History—1953- —Fiction. I. Title.
PQ2637.I547I513   1991   843'.914—dc20   91-7905
ISBN: 0-916583-79-1 (cloth)
ISBN: 0-916583-90-2 (paper)

First paperback edition, 1992

Partially funded by grants from The National Endowment for the Arts and
The Illinois Arts Council.

Dalkey Archive Press
1817 North 79th Avenue
Elmwood Park, IL 60635 USA

Printed on permanent/durable acid-free paper and bound in the United States of America.

The only permanent factor in history is geography.

—Bismarck

Ordinarily (that is to say, since their arrival in the country, ten days before) they were all driven, each accompanied by an interpreter, in private cars, the large black kind that has gathered curtains stretched across the rear window, but this time they were ushered into a bus which, in the wake of a police car, not traveling at any excessive speed, though still not neglecting to run the light at every intersection, finally arrived in front of an ordinary-looking building and the fifteen passengers were invited to leave the bus. One behind the other they passed through the door, crossed a vestibule, climbed two flights of stairs, walked along a corridor, and emerged in the chamber where the secretary-general awaited them.

Perhaps one or more uniformed guards stood outside, as is usual at the entrances of official buildings, but no one noticed them, at least not any more than one notices the porters or doormen of a hotel (the same brown uniforms trimmed with red or blue braid, the same caps, the same vacant, disinterested airs) when one gets out of a taxi on the way to an important meeting. In the vestibule and on the stairway, directing them or watching them pass, were men who looked like functionaries or bailiffs, dressed in sober grey suits, mostly young, efficient-looking, discreet, the type that one meets everywhere in such places: ministries, the residences of heads of state, or headquarters of important organizations.

The fifteen guests formed an incongruous group, with an average age of about sixty, of diverse nationalities and professions; there were some among them (the youngest in particular, a Mediterranean) who carried themselves with a studied elegance, others (one of whom walked with the aid of a cane) whose appearance (their attire and physique) was entirely anonymous, both stilted and slightly fatigued though satisfied, like those participants of international conferences or meetings that one can always find in press photos; the group (as a justification, as it were, of its existence or perhaps simply to add an element of decoration, of the exotic) included three personages who differed from the others not only in the color of their skin but also in their dress, the most conspicuous of whom had the head of a Nubian gladiator that looked as though it were cast in bronze, a straight nose, fine though slightly fleshy features, dazzling teeth. He wore a tunic and straight, sky blue trousers, a long sash of white cotton draped across his torso, his chest decorated on one side by one of those medals of honor that generals wear; the two others (two brothers) resembled those evangelical preachers or rather one of those black duos just as capable of singing as of playing the trumpet or of setting their feet to snapping and cracking in the spotlight of a music hall; they were entirely dressed in somber colors, from their narrow tap shoes to the turtleneck sweaters on which their ebony heads seemed balanced as though they had been decapitated, slightly thrown back, as though held by a chin strap or a neck brace, pivoting, however, with that quickness or rather that suddenness that one sees in birds and, for the moment, directed toward the left while, filing along with their companions, they turned, one after the other, immediately to the right after having stepped through the doorway situated at the end and to one side of a chamber of average size, like the meeting room of a board of directors, longer than wide, in the center of which stood a table of the same proportions on which glasses and bottles of mineral water were arranged at each place, the majestic Nubian gladiator still draped in his immaculate toga was the third to enter, the elegant Mediterranean diplomat advancing first, walking the length of the table and arriving, finally, at its end where stood, slightly back from the table, the personage who had invited them.

There were no introductions. Perhaps the secretary (or the writer who had sent out the letters of invitation?), standing in place beside the host, whispered to him the name of each of the guests as they shook his hand. Or perhaps not. Perhaps he didn't concern himself about it (that is to say, about the identity or the name of any of them in particular: it was probably sufficient that they were there, that someone had told him that these were the men whose names were well known in their countries), perhaps he had quickly read over the list in advance (the list on which was included, among others, besides the black duo and the magnificent Nubian gladiator, an actor who had re-created the role of Nero in the movies and the second husband of the most beautiful woman in the world) or simply asked for a brief report from his aides (he had just returned from a meeting with the other head of state who could also, with one word, destroy half the world: another actor, a man who had attained this position not by virtue of any special capacities or knowledge but by galloping on a horse, wearing a cowboy hat and grinning from ear to ear, in B movies). Thus, for a moment only the shuffling of shoes along the floor was heard as, guided by the functionaries, the fifteen guests, having walked the length of the table once, walked its length again in the opposite direction, those who entered first circling its other end crossing again the distance between the door and the man they had just met, each taking a place, immobile, in front of a chair, waiting until the last had taken their places in turn at the other side of the table, then, at a gesture from their host and in imitation of him, pulling the chairs to them, seating themselves, the muffled scraping of the chairs' rubber padded feet across the floor barely having died out when the man who could destroy half the world was already speaking in a soft, affable, even jovial voice, welcoming his guests.

L ong after the last pealing notes from the brasses had echoed through the house, after the last roll of the timpani had died out, after the curtain had fallen, the auditorium—five tiers of balconies all in white and gold in the shape of a horseshoe, boxes with seats upholstered in purple velvet, gigantic chandelier—continued to reverberate with the sound of applause, like the din of hail on a roof, drowning out everything else, submerging the cries of bravo that came from here and there, weakening, resuming, swelling anew, filling the enormous nave with a monstrous roaring, vaguely disquieting, like the thundering of those untamed cataracts where millions of tons of water tip and plunge over the edge, almost menacing, and above which the cheers redoubled seeming like cries of distress, of alarm, of fury even, each time that the curtain rose again and the tiny silhouette in the wan shaft of the spotlight advanced to the center of the stage, like a phantom apparition whose glow, it seemed, could be coming as easily from its own luminous substance as from the light of the beam shining upon it: not flesh, muscles, and skin but formed, it seemed, of some phosphorescent material, its contours imprecise, blurred, nebulous, creating not so much the outline of a body, an iridescent form wrapped in silk, as a succession of poses: bowing, bending a knee, gracefully gathering up one of the bouquets which, like eccentric projectiles, seemed to leap from here and there catapulted by springs hidden in the tumultuous darkness, and to scatter in the garish glow of the footlights surrounding the prima ballerina, her face upturned, raised toward the flies, her arms held out before her, palms open, bowing once more, then disappearing, the heavy blood-colored curtain closing again, its heavy fringes crashing silently together, rebounding, like waves, twisting backward on themselves, rejoining, then hovering, quivering for a moment before coming to rest, the applause and the clamor now diminishing, the fifteen

guests continuing, however, to hear them, far offstage, growing fitful, dying out, then coming again, swelling up again,
demanding, while they were led through a labyrinth of
columns, of white marble, of stairways and galleries where
the inconsolable phantoms of deceased chamberlains and
grand duchesses seemed to wander, finally passing through a
door beyond which there suddenly opened a space lacking
both limits and precise dimensions, that is to say, with the
exception of the vast dusty floor and a lowered stage curtain
(dusty and grey itself on this side) illuminated by the blinding
light from some electric bulbs hung here and there, lost in
the indistinct shadows vaguely inhabited by cardboard
bushes, frames, cobwebbed backdrops, waving feebly in the
musty currents that also, now and then, caused the immense
curtain, through which the sputtering of the last curtain call
reached again, to billow out, nearer now but as though from
another world, the last applause no longer a solid mass of
sound but staccato now, though obstinate, growing more
ragged, little by little breaking apart, as it were, splintering,
less and less sustained, then, at last, ceasing, giving way—
though they (the fifteen guests) had begun to hear it as they
had passed through the door that gave access to the wings—
to the tranquil cacophony of hammer blows and of things
banging together or dragged along that reigns over demoli-
tion sites or areas where some disaster, natural or not, has
occurred; and in the midst of which—grey herself, as though
also covered with (or rather made of, materialized from and
ready to return to) that dust which seemed, like a rain of
ashes, to have fallen indifferently on the sets, the fake muslin
clouds, the fake moonlight, the stagehands, the floor—the old
woman stood, a bouquet of withered flowers in the crook of

her arm: a midget almost, fragile in her gossamer dust-colored veils, exhausted, her shoulders hastily covered with one of those crocheted shawls worn by concierges or the residents of nursing homes.

He would never have thought that she was so old. Even after everything that he had been told about her. Even when he saw her, phosphorescent in the haze of light, through those little opera glasses left at their disposal (with the plates of tea biscuits and the inevitable bottles of mineral water which, in this setting, had something comic, something derisive about them) on the table in the reception room at the rear of the loge—the royal box, at the center of the second balcony, furnished with large gilt armchairs upholstered with the same velvet as the backdrops, the same armchairs (they dated apparently from the middle of the preceding century, restored to their original gold not by real leaf but with the aid of inexpensive imitation gold paint) where emperors and bejeweled empresses had certainly been seated, where, now when he came, one of the two most powerful men in the world would sit, where, before him, doddering old men had sat, and before the old men, the man with the bandit mustache, with the paternal smile of a bandit, with the philosophy and the morals of a murderer and who, because of ambition, cruelty, amusement, fear, or simple stupidity, had had arrested, beaten, condemned, sent to prison, and put to death, with or without a verdict, human beings, men and women, infants and the aged, by the million, he too sat there on gala days, his bravos, his off-color jokes, his frowns anxiously watched for or rather kept on the lookout for by those who were the closest to him, seated at his side (trembling, fearing) in the other gilt armchairs while with those same opera glasses

13

made of mother-of-pearl or of ivory ringed with brass, he watched unfold on that very stage something roughly similar to what they (the fifteen guests) had just seen, that is to say, something which to the mind of a poor seminarian (which he had been before becoming a bandit) without a doubt had to represent the ineffable summit of beauty, grace, and harmony, that which forty years after his death his successors had continued, and continued still—as though under the influence of some Shakespearean terror or superstition (there had been laws for that, decrees, detailed directives founded on punctilious philosophical gibberish regulating, to the smallest detail, the method for blowing into a cornet as well as how to hold a paintbrush)—to assign as a goal, as the raison d'être for the dancers, for the musicians, and for the painters of the scenery.

And perhaps this same—that is to say, the one who was now a grande dame, so old that she must have performed, on these same dusty boards, though just an unknown young dancer then, or perhaps already a rising star on the horizon, the same swooning gestures, to bow her head, to smile, to pirouette, flexing and relaxing her muscles of iron to the accompaniment of the clamorous applause of the bandit with the name of iron, to maintain the same elegant pose, the same graceful curve of her arms (younger then than at present) suspended from the flies by an invisible steel cable, her weakening legs concealed by a cardboard cloud, rising and falling at the mercy of an arrangement of pulleys, she was content with gracefully waving her pale, emaciated, powdered arms in imitation of the wings of a wounded gull, bending, bowing her head first to one side and then to the other to the plaintive sounds of the orchestra's flutes, then, returning from her heaven, supported or rather carried by a robust partner, weakly demonstrating, back arched, calves stretched taut, exhausted and pathetic, the leaps that had been her glory, for which she had received, from the hands of heads of state in all the capital cities, as many illustrious decorations, ribbons, crosses, medals, and laurels as a victorious general, and disappearing finally in the tempest of bravos and the thunder of timpani that accented the pistol shot that threw the body of her partner onto the proscenium rolling over several times until he lay, his arms crossed, his head bent back touching the footlights, the public already standing, the tumult, the cheers bursting out, the Nubian gladiator in his magnificent sky blue tunic also on his feet tossing his cotton toga over his shoulder, beating his hands together clamorously, the uproar at its peak, the cheers, the thundering applause continuing to rise up from the orchestra, from the balconies, with that unusual, alarming quality, heard everywhere, in the cries wrenched from human beings or from animals by an excess of pleasure, of sadness, of fury, or of fear.

And after that, nothing. Nothing but the vast space with imprecise limits, the dust-covered set, grey, already surrendered to the stagehands whose hammer blows resounded, losing themselves in echoes of the cold, vague gloom. As though even before the applause had stopped, even before the dancers had finished taking their bows, the spotlights no sooner extinguished, the curtain no sooner lowered on the enchanted spectacle (the spectacle, the thundering ballet that on the absinthe-colored posters bore the same name in Cyrillic letters as the play written some hundred years earlier by the gentle myopic indulging his melancholy, his thinness, his goatee, his pince-nez, and his unhealthy lungs under the

15

Claude Simon

palm trees and in the shade of spas and seaside resorts from
one end of Europe to the other, sick herself, erasing each line,
each silence, allowing nothing of the roles that he entrusted
to the actors to exist on the page except traces of murmurs,
whispers: Europe, the old continent of philosophers, musicians, and painters of hazy suns, withered and out of date,
governed by monarchs who wore goatees or side whiskers,
gentlemen wearing opera hats, and which was about to be
shaken by something thunderous, more monstrous than the
blast of brass and the rolling drums . . .) than the stagehands
were, at a command, already engaged in making disappear, as
quickly as possible, even the smallest trace of the scenery, as
though nothing could be allowed to remain of the fake trees,
the fake bushes, the benches and the lawn chairs, of the
romantic light of the moon, the clouds, and that she (the old
lady, the former star who could leap like a deer, the past glory
of the times of the seminarian, she who was no more now to
dance than a voiceless singer is to song) might fulfill the
second part of her role (of her destiny?): the part that she
could still play without other support than that of her ward-
robe mistress almost as old as she, standing at her side like the
confidante in a tragedy (the tragedy, the tragic which the
beats of the bass drum and the deafening brasses of the
orchestra had vainly tried to equal), that is to say, she stood,
gaunt and terrifying, in the midst of the immense empty
plateau, the periphery of which was lost in the gloom: like a
queen abandoned, some barbarian idol, holding herself erect
with the last of her strength, beyond fatigue, still trying to
catch her breath, her chest, the knobby ladder of her breast-
bone exposed by the décolleté of her bodice, rising and falling
rapidly, the expression of one bewildered and lost on her

16

face, as though the agony that she had acted remained, the
mask fallen, her eyes like those of a small, hunted animal
ringed with dark halos formed by the stage makeup smeared
by her perspiration, and finding still the strength to smile
while surrounded by the fifteen guests each of whose hands
she shook one after the other, listening (or not listening) to
the compliments, thanking them with the same weary,
mechanical smile, her face furrowed by lines as deep as the
wrinkles of faces ruined by greasepaint, like cardboard, as
though the life had been sucked out a long time ago, her eyes
brilliant with that glitter that only tears can give—or perhaps
the reflection of the nearest blinding electric light bulb
gently swinging in the air currents, alternately elongating or
contracting the shadows on the small, crumpled mask, not
much larger than the face of an infant mummy, ashen, the
cheekbones kept alive with a trace of rouge.

For a long time there had been nothing to see but the
moon, not completely full, her left side slightly flat-
tened, milky, or rather, silvery, like a lantern which
seemed to float along at the same speed as the airplane, as
though welded to it, rising or falling a little sometimes, then
taking her place again, or rather as though the plane and she
were held immobile, suspended without advancing through
the starless night while thousands of meters below them the
monstrous stretches of earth by which two continents were
attached drifted slowly, invisible in the obscurity, two worlds
not face-to-face on each side of some sea, or some shifting

ocean, but stuck together, one to the other, like those bi-
cephalous creatures, those Siamese twins exhibited in fair
booths, welded back-to-back, condemned never to see each
other though all the while breathing or digesting through
some common organ, indivisible, hypertrophic, elephantine
(and on the way back, in the daylight, they would see that,
that is to say, the opposite of fluidity, of movement: for
several hours something uniformly ocher, uniformly flat,
above which hung parallel chains of small, round clouds,
immobile, paired with their shadows, also immobile, with
lakes here and there, or rather ponds, already covered,
though it was only October, with a film of ice, and without a
city, without a hamlet, without a farm, without a road, not
even a path, streaked from west to east only by a railway line
that stretched until lost from sight, absolutely rectilinear,
without a hill to skirt, without even the meanderings of a
valley to follow, drawn straight, coming from nowhere and
leading nowhere: a scab, an immense dead expanse, empty,
definitively infertile, and definitively immobile).

And finally (the plane had already been flying three hours
—the plane specially chartered for the fifteen guests, their
fifteen interpreters, and the five or six attendants whose true
purpose, be it to take care of them, to watch them, or to watch
each other while among them, no one knew for sure—the
airplane, whose departure they had awaited for almost two
hours (after having already waited about an hour (which
makes three altogether: as though the waiting (because of
mysterious orders, annulled by counterorders no less mysterious, themselves annulled in their turn) made up, as it were,
an essential and intransgressible part of the established
program) in the middle of the main hall of the building with

the imperial columns, with the moquette carpeting and with the few threadbare chairs, the bus that would take them) in the luxurious lounge of the deserted nocturnal airport (the typical prefab luxury, garish and cheap, such as the designers of airports all over the world conceive it, with the difference that this decor had something naïvely pompous about it: the marble, the fake oriental carpets, like a color catalog from some big department store, the chandeliers, the glass tables and the brass ashtrays) seated, however, now in the deep armchairs, always watched (or attended) by their escorts who, grouped standing around the one who seemed to be the leader, and absorbed in one of their eternal confabulations, interrupting, breaking off their conversation each time that one of the black duo stood up, crossed the length of the vast hall with his dancing gait, swinging his hips, letting his hands sway gracefully from his wrists, around which he had knotted a silk scarf, while passing his bluish tongue over his lower lip, disappearing for a moment, then reappearing, returning to seat himself on the settee where his brother waited for him, their two sharp voices rising again, the chief escort pulling himself together, the twenty pairs of eyes turning, one or another of the young interpreters still continuing to glance incredulously in the direction of the settee from which from time to time loud and incomprehensible bursts of laughter would break out, the two economists and the Mediterranean diplomat who had pulled their chairs together also lifted their heads casting a rapid glance at the duo, one of them also furtively looking at the time on his wrist and then at the group of escorts, still huddled together, and taking up the interrupted conversation again, the murmur of voices barely audible, patient, cheerless, punctuated at intervals by explosions of

19

Claude Simon

laughter, the gorgeous Nubian gladiator still draped in his
toga, seated alone, his imperial bronze visage impassive, his
bronze lips closed on the stem of a pipe from which he drew
slow puffs, the night advancing, the long white fuselages of
airplanes on the other side of the glazed partition still immobile, without any apparent preparations, until finally there
was some movement of a sort by one of the doors, the group
of escorts broke up, dispersed, each approaching his guest to
have him board the plane) ... and finally, because the clouds
that hid the earth had broken up, or because the airplane had
passed through the expanse of these black solitudes, lacking
any trace of life, a vague glow appeared on the right growing
little by little, not announced by those isolated outposts, those
scatterings of light which habitually surround cities, multiply-
ing little by little, closing ranks, regrouping until becoming
one, but a block, that is to say, a clearly defined stain, closed,
shut in upon itself, so to speak, the light itself not blurred, surrounded by a halo formed of vaporous air, but carving the
night with that categorical precision seen in the contours of
arid regions, as though inert, without those glitterings or
seethings, those fiery lava flows which cities seen from on
high sometimes resemble, but fixed, frozen, rigid, in the midst
of or rather within the bounds of the darkness (and what
name?: there were none of those maps that are usually found
in seatback pockets and on which one can follow the path of
the flight indicated in red: only some tourist brochures showing girls in folk costumes in the cotton fields, flowery parks,
some steel castings and theaters made of reinforced cement:
something no doubt like one of those names evoking silk,
carpets, and minarets—unless it was the name of an industrial
complex), growing slowly in the night, solitary, at the foot of

some formidable mountains, at the crossroads of some formidable and invisible deserts, the interior of the cabin filled with
nasal voices (the voices of Harlem, Madrid, or Calcutta but all
speaking the same language, the idiom used indiscriminately
by bleach-blond stars, bellhops, and the dealers of everything
in the world that can be bought or sold from automobiles to
stretch pants by way of carbonated drinks alcoholic or not)
raised to be heard above the powerful rushing of air against
the fuselage of the airplane, the expanse of icy air, black,
formidable, stretching above the enigmatic pool of gold that
continued to drift on the sea of darkness, sliding off on the
right, little by little, diminishing, and then again, nothing,
blackness, the nasal jabbering of voices (the fabulous gladiator
in his fabulous general's uniform chewing pieces of eel or
smoked tongue placed on his tray while explaining to his
neighbor (he also explained that he had studied at Oxford)
that he was a painter, that is to say, an artist, that is to say (he
pushed his tray away, bent over, fumbled in his elegant traveling bag, and drew a box of slides from it), that he has painted
the portraits of all the leaders of his country, holding, one after
the other, a procession of pictures of men with bronze or
black faces up to the light, dressed in the same exotic outfits,
behind them skies just before dawn or just before a storm,
streaked with sinuous trails of flamboyant pink and purple
(he does not say if it was also at Oxford that he had learned to
paint in this style—although seeing the style (recalling that
of those full-length portraits of sovereigns and princes
consort in their ceremonial robes or dressed for polo) it
seemed probable), the same skies, the same fiery clouds (or
banners?) serving as indiscriminately as a background to
peasants bent over their archaic plows, to blacksmiths, or to

shepherds), a second island of light appearing, still on the
right, still homogeneous, glowing with the same fixed
brilliance growing in its turn (he (the painter in the general's
uniform) seemed to have painted everything that he could in
his own country, had even designed (he showed them, slides
too, commenting on each picture volubly in his perfect
English, inexhaustible, smiling, showing his gleaming teeth)
the postage stamps, in a manner, he explained, necessarily
more stylized and in which, in different colors, the same
weavers, potters, and the same shepherds were harmoniously
combined on the small rectangles, green, yellow, or lilac,
with a hammer and sickle, also stylized), then several small
islands of light floating like an archipelago, seeming at
present to rise up to meet the plane, then tilting, disappearing, then reappearing again, closer, the noise of the engines,
the beating of the air outside the cabin different, then the
lights shooting rapidly past at the same height as the airplane,
very quickly, fleeing, the plane rolling now, shaking with
gentle vibrations, slowing again, turning, finally stopping,
and, when the door was opened, the night air suddenly, pure,
fresh—not cold: fresh—the lights that lit the airport building
revealing on the runway a confusion of obscure silhouettes,
the fifteen guests descending the gangway one after the
other, sleepily, sluggish, in that state of semiconsciousness
reached by revelers after a sleepless night, offering their
hands automatically, their arms shaken vigorously by a
person with massive head and shoulders, in the dark, repeat-
ing for each of them the same massive words of welcome and
of friendship, immediately translated by the interpreter
whose voice continued its mechanical delivery in each of the
automobiles in which they now sat, eyelids drooping and

burning, limbs heavy, hearing, without listening, the chain of
words in which they did not try to find any meaning, delivered
with that mixture of obstinacy, of indifference, and of stub-
born conviction that one finds in children who are made to
recite fables, used-car salesmen, or nurses assigned to hope-
less cases, the sound of the feeble voice like a sonorous background, struggling to fill up the waiting (car doors slammed
shut one after the other, now long ago, the chauffeur's seat
still empty, in any case, the row of automobiles still immobile
on the runway next to the plane now with its lights extinguished, as though the journey had to be set off, before the
departure and after the arrival, by a sort of margin, a dead
time, and finally again (in the east the sky began to lighten)
there were calls, orders outside, at the same time as the
shadowy figures wearing military hats surged into the lead
vehicle, the chauffeur (a person who looked as though he
slaughtered sheep or broke wild horses, with an open collar,
dressed in informal jacket and pants) getting in, slamming in
turn his door and putting the car in gear), the feeble voice,
insipid, rising an octave to be heard over the noise of the
engine, and the dawn now breaking in earnest, the darkness
withdrawing little by little, as though regretting it, like an
alluvial stream leaving an even grey mud behind it, shadowy
shreds still lingering, letting the forms of the poplars border-
ing the straight road along which the convoy of automobiles
rolled emerge, the light still uncertain, at that moment when
things have no color, revealing on the steppes shepherds
mounted on their small ponies, small gardens here and there
along the road, cottages with whitewashed walls, with grey
roofs, the countryside awakening, becoming populated little
by little (or rather already awake: yellow lights showing in

Claude Simon

the windows of the small houses, shadowy figures trudging
along the roadside, already congregating in long lines where
the heavy buses dragged their sagging loads on the high-
ways), the small houses and cottages growing more numerous,
the horizon blotched by something chaotic, formidable,
pearly grey at first, indistinct, like an accumulation of clouds,
then, suddenly, above the poplars, the shepherds on their
small ponies, the cottages flooded in the half-light, touched
by the first light of the sun, shining suddenly, with angles,
planes, facets, like a shattering of diamonds, the snow throwing its icy fires, monstrous, immobile: now the column of
heavy automobiles preceded by the police car passed through
the city (the city, sprung from the steppe, in which the language had once been Chinese, then Chinese transcribed first
into roman characters, then a second time into Cyrillic, the
city in which not counting some dozens of dialects (dialects
of the sons of camel drivers, Mongolian horsemen, inhabitants
descended from the towering mountains, the caravanners:
Tartars, Afghans, Kirghizes, Turkistanis, Uzbeks, the former
slaves, the new arrivals—there was even, the interpreter said,
a colony of Germans . . .) two languages are now officially
spoken, both written in Cyrillic characters) which sixty years
before had been nothing but a large primitive village (or
even less, perhaps: a stopover, a halt at the end of the interminable steppes and before the terrifying passes of the
mountains) and in which live now close to a million people of
all races, with yellow skin or not, with slanted eyes or not (or
slightly slanted, or with slightly too-prominent cheekbones),
and who at that hour could be seen bustling in the early dawn
in hurrying crowds on both sides of the colossal avenues
planted with trees at the foot of cement grillwork facades,

24

advancing, without looking at them, past the ever-present heavy red cotton banners with the incomprehensible injunctions hung throughout the parks and the squares, squeezing into already-crammed buses (now the colors can be seen: they were yellow, dented and dusty, spewing, when starting up, a cloud of black smoke) stopped at the intersections by the police to allow the guests' cortege to pass, the tires squealing around the curves, going at full speed past peristyle monuments, columns, pediments, erected there, in the heart of the monstrous continent of steppes and mountains, around esplanades, forums, wide malls and squares, the whole thing emerged, completed, as it stands, three thousand kilometers away from the drawings of some state-licensed architect, an orientalist, megalomaniac, and philanthropist, to the glory of the fiery bronze rider whose statue rose in the main square and who had given his own name to the city like the rustling and snapping of a flag.

Then, as abruptly as they had appeared, the ostentatious structures disappeared, giving place to the whitewashed cottages surrounded by small garden plots, and shortly thereafter the automobiles slowed, and finally stopped. And then this (that is to say, still as the senses perceive everything after a sleepless night: separate, isolated one from the other, in a woolly unreality, vaguely unbelievable): in the fresh morning, pearl grey, on the steps of something that resembled a museum (something also made of concrete, but faced with marble), a slightly plump personage, wearing a pearl grey suit, sporting a discreetly striped pearl grey silk tie, smiling from ear to ear, bowing ceremoniously in the Asian fashion, his face round, flat, smooth, and yellow, slanting eyes, he too speaking in an incomprehensible language, showing with a

grand gesture the steps of the porch (and very close now,
sparkling in the first rays of the sun, the huge barrier of snow
and ice), then the marble staircase, then opening the door
not of a chamber but of a suite with the same mail-order
oriental carpets and furniture, of mahogany, leather, and
brass, as though the complete stock had been transported,
standing lamps, ruffled lamp shades, and pedestals included,
from one of those department stores that specialize in inlaid
pieces, the bronzes and the carpets of Chinese manufacture,
the chauffeur (the sheep slaughterer) setting down the
visitor's valises, the traveler, finally alone, contemplating the
stereotypical decor around him in bewilderment, the sprays
of flowers, the monumental pyramid of fruit on one of the
tables, opening one after the other the doors of the two rooms,
the two bathrooms, incredulous, somnambulistic. There was
a terrace with a table, rattan chairs, and a woven carpet, red
and green. The sound of an invisible torrent could be heard
beyond a curtain of poplars that autumn had yellowed and
whose leaves stirred feebly. The air was dry and calm. On the
other side of the torrent two small people slowly followed a
path parallel to its bed that ascended the first slopes of the
mountain, the monstrous rising up of the earth, the monstrous
roof of the world at the foot of which the steppes stopped, the
monstrous sheets of snow and ice succeeding each other in
waves superimposed one upon the other, cut by calcified
plateaus, into the unbreathable air, to the already-formidable
foothills without tree or a bush, reddish brown, arid, bare,
formidable, silent, deserted.

The Invitation

Along the walls parallel to the table, on the side that the fifteen guests skirted as they entered, were small cubicles separated from each other by wooden partitions in each of which an interpreter was seated translating simultaneously in a different language the words of the secretary-general that the guests could follow with headphones, paying, to tell the truth, less attention at first (or in any case, certain among them) to the words themselves than they did to the speaker, studying with curiosity the face that millions of televisions and millions of photographs had, a little more than a year ago, already made familiar to the entire world: still young, round, with delicate features, an intelligent expression (inasmuch as he was speaking with that mixture of charm, firmness, good faith, and duplicity inherent in all statesmen, face and voice—although it was actually the translators' voices—eventually blending, becoming only one), and the appearance, bald, a sober navy blue jacket and tasteful tie, of the youngest descendant of a line of gangsters who had been educated in a Swiss college (with the difference that he had not been raised in Switzerland but that he had raised himself, helped only by his own strength, in the heart of a jungle where the only law was trickery and violence—which implied a real talent for the use of either one or the other) and who, upon returning home after his studies at the institute in the canton of Vaud where billionaires and gangsters had their progeny trained, had undertaken to redirect the affairs of the family into reputable and honorable businesses, that is to say, less precarious, less naively brutal, and more profitable business than street hits and mass deportations: something more elaborate, as it were, something with stock that could be quoted on international markets, the slow asphyxiation by

27

silicon of Chilean miners, for example, or the discreet exter-
mination of Asian women in textile mills. His instinct coupled
with his powers of observation helped him to see that what
he needed above all else, at least as a front, was respectability,
an imperative that demanded first that certain actions or
attitudes be avoided, showing restraint (like not putting up
statues of yourself at every intersection, not having poems to
your glory written), and that some actions be taken (for he
must have read somewhere that no Texan billionaire, no
matter how rich he might be, was allowed to join the blue
blood's club of his town if he had not first donated a museum
—or at least a collection), like showing an interest, being
disinterested, so to speak, concerning uninteresting people
and things, that is to say, without any immediate influence,
nevertheless, probably never having had the time to read
enough for himself (and, moreover, probably not worrying
himself about it), he was obliged to rely on the counselors
who themselves had only a confused idea about them and
who relied on the habitual criteria of their kind of people, the
same in all countries, choosing a little by chance, blindly,
depending on those (the criteria) of complacency or of
notoriety like that, for example, which having a black skin can
confer, having played the role of Nero in the movies, or
received a coveted international distinction, which explained
the heterogeneous composition of the group of fifteen guests
whom he now addressed, with that affability, that courtesy,
and that incommensurable contempt which generally every
man of action holds for those who, with or without justification, make a profession of thinking, he who with a word could
unleash an apocalypse, have a nation invaded, name or ruin
heads of state, who, unobtrusive, attentive, prudent, biding

his time, had patiently climbed the echelons of that hier-
archy, or rather of that dangerous secret society, closed in on
itself, where the least mistake in the observance of custom,
the slightest error in judgment irremediably entailed death,
if not physical (it has been some time now since, following a
sort of a gentleman's—if one may use that term—agreement,
the gang leaders repudiated that method of elimination
among themselves) at least of all hope, using his intelligence
to maneuver between police reports and subtle balances of
influence, ratifying absurd or brutal decisions, yielding to
absurd rites of precedence, temporizing, cautious, never
ceasing to watch what went on around him, reflecting on the
means of obtaining power for himself, but also, on that which
was of primary importance if he wanted to maintain himself
in power, that (the means) of bringing millions of people
from the ancestral status of beasts of burden to that of produc-
tive beings, and, to achieve this without absolutely having (he
had also traveled abroad, there too observing attentively how
things were done) to beat them or have them shot, in such a
way that it was necessary for him to succeed in convincing
not only these (and without a doubt himself primarily) but
moreover the rest of the world that looked at him askance,
that he was no different than any normal man (if in fact one
may use that term for the kings of the automobile, of ham-
burger, or of canned pork—but if after all, the world needs
other things besides automobiles, hamburgers, and canned
pork), that is to say, that no suspicious bulge swelled his
jacket where a pistol could be hidden and that, in the position
he had held, it was possible that a fairly normal man could
have followed a succession of bandits straight out of, one
could say, disguised by their uniform of floppy hats and stiff

gabardines, the distant beginnings of History, with the difference that the heads of predatory beasts or monsters formerly
painted on the coats of arms or shields (the heads of wild boars,
the heads of foxes, of jackals, wolves, of hippopotamuses, or
of rats) appeared on them wedged between the band of the
inevitable felt hat (or of the inevitable astrakhan) pulled
down over the eyes and a starched collar, the eyes themselves uniformly fixed, absent, empty, dead, as expressive as
the buttons on a boot or grains of slag: these same eyes, the
same vacant insensible stares that when, a little after the
death of the bandit seminarian, they (the men with rats',
hippopotamuses', or jackals' heads) had reopened the door of
the Council Chamber in which they had met, and, without a
word, with a simple movement of the head, showed the body,
stretched out on the floor, of the man whom they had just
assassinated to the astonished guards: something (the episode
—what should one call it?: the drama, the Shakespearean
scene, the murder, the execution? the boxing match? . . .)
arising not even then from the stutterings of History, from its
stammerings, but from its wailing—and not savage, barbarous,
but precisely animal, that is to say, necessity not by calculation,
ambition, but the simple and primitive instinct of preservation:
and even then without weapons, no daggers, no clubs (it was
precisely for that reason that they had chosen this place:
because no one—not even he before whom they trembled
with fear, the boss of the seminarian's killers—had the right
to enter there armed or with his guards): with bare hands
then—and how they did it no one ever knew: one of them
waiting for him perhaps behind the door, throwing himself
on him, tackling him—or stunning him with a chair—or
gagging him immediately with a handkerchief, throwing a

The Invitation

rug over his head (one version of the story has it that the body had been carried out rolled in a carpet), the other bandits with animal heads hurling themselves at him at the same time, crushing him beneath their weight, in a heap, striking out blindly, smothering that which could be smothered, smashing that which could be smashed in the body that struggled, twisting his arms, scratching his face, his throat, clawing, all in silence: only the growls, the grunts, the smothered howls, and finally, when he stopped struggling, getting up, panting, their hands still trembling, readjusting their clothes, looking for their glasses on the ground, straightening their ties, putting the furniture back in place, dusting themselves off, discussing in low voices, assuring themselves one last time that he was in fact dead, perhaps giving him one last kick, and finally one of them deciding, walking to the door, opening it wide and, merely gesturing to the guards, indicating the cadaver of the man who, some minutes before, had entered full of life, perhaps some pleasantry on his lips (the kind of joke that freezes whoever is the butt of it with terror, the lips tight, malicious, terrifying, his malicious eyes, intelligent, also terrifying behind the elegant spectacles of an intellectual, the regular face, aristocratic, which could as easily have been that of a grand duke as a department head in a large store), and from this moment on continuing to behave outwardly like wolves, jackals, or hippopotamuses, violently crushing anyone who tried to lift his head but wary of each other, still, after thirty years of permanent terror and of permanent insecurity, with a memory of panic and, after having favored him with some honorific title, to banish in turn one after another of them (the hippopotamus first, then one or two of the foxes, the one who had the head of a Pekingese

31

dog) to the heart of the impenetrable desert, taking great care not to disturb that fragile equilibrium between brute force and that philosophical potpourri that permitted them to preside over the military parades, applaud graceful ballets and, while climbing the steps to airplanes that would take them to international conferences, exhibit for the press photographers the same faces always closed, peevish, and set wedged into the eternal floppy felt hats and the eternal gabardines.

And now (it was a little more than a year since the previous secretary-general had been put into the earth, since every television in the world had transmitted (that of the country and those of the neighboring countries, vassal states or more or less subordinated, from start to finish) the images of the interminable ceremony, since millions of men and women fascinated or curious (or simply indifferent, quickly tired, turning the dial) had been able to see the final parade, the coffin drawn all along the interminable route beneath a grey sky through the streets of the capital: the open coffin that let a flaccid face appear in the midst of a mountain of red flowers, crowned by white hair a lock of which was sometimes lifted by the wind, the hearse surrounded by six guards (three on each side) or rather six giants, six elite officers capable of violently throwing their stiff booted legs high out in front with each step without weakening for several miles, as stiff themselves as robots, to the slow cadence of the romantic funeral march replayed a hundred times—it was a little more than a year ago (but it seemed distant already) that the widow had bent (or rather she had been helped to bend, supported: she was herself very old) over the face with closed eyes to kiss it one last time, to make the sign of the cross above it before the lid was closed, the monotonous and interminable ranks of soldiers, with fixed bayonets, their faces parallel simultaneously turned to the right filing past him, and on the other side of the square (the square, the immense paved desert, bulging slightly, naked without a fountain, without a statue, without any other ornament except at one side the stone platform on which the condemned were tortured and the church with variegated bell towers, twining, turbaned, or cut like diamonds, the pavement along which processions of long-bearded priests had crowded, dressed in gold, balancing censers, chanting psalms in their deep, bass voices, where the dreams of glory of a conquerer surrounded by plumed marshals, eagles, and an army which spoke all the languages of Europe had come to die . . .) the files of elite guards, without weapons, juvenile, looking like schoolboys drawn up in battle ranks, shouting out three times their cry of farewell drowned out by the music that continued to play, so that one saw only the hundreds of mouths opening and closing in silence, like fishes' mouths, each time (because winter was approaching and it was already cold) letting little clouds of vapor escape. The bust of the new secretary-general now cut by the parapet at the top of the red marble cube in the square where before him so many old men had stood, escorted by the highest dignitaries with, immediately to his left, looking at him, a man wearing a fur hat and a thoughtful expression, ravaged, the manner of a tired old wolf (or rather not exactly old: simply ravaged—not exactly interested: simply thoughtful), the new secretary-general, bareheaded, bald, his features astonishingly young, almost babylike, examined, evaluated by millions of men and women, diplomats, journalists, makers of hypotheses) . . . and now, seated at the head of that table

Claude Simon

which resembled that of an ordinary board of directors of a
joint stock company perhaps, or perhaps not, of an international bank perhaps, or perhaps not, with its polished surface
like a mirror, its glasses and bottles of mineral water, in the
room with bare walls, without a portrait, neither of his prede-
cessors nor of himself, he . . .

During all the time that they spent at the foot of the
formidable mountain they heard the torrent. It was
there, invisible, hidden in the ravine where the
poplars grew, out of reach on the other side of the impassable
fence that surrounded the grounds of the luxurious houses,
and from the sound, the incessant and tumultuous roar, one
could imagine it, frothing, the waters leaping up, hurtling
down endlessly, emerging from some fantastic glacier and
pouring out finally onto the plain (the plain, the parched
steppe where it lost itself) having broken out of the confining
gorges, rushing down from cataract to cataract, still furious,
snorting, shaking its watery mane, black and silver, endlessly
gathering its liquid tresses, seething, as though the voice of
some monster, some mocking oracle, relentlessly reached
down from the old and monstrous mountain as a heavy bel-
lowing, indifferent, the bearer of some secret without secret.
  Little by little they grew used to each other, each to the
others as well as to their situation, that is to say, they no longer
followed the undulating walk of the older pastor with astonished gazes, no more surprised by his iridescent silk scarves
and blue tongue than by caviar on their plates even at break-

fast, by the yellow-skinned servants (some more yellow than others) in pearl grey uniforms, with dazzling white shirt-fronts, bow ties and worn-out shoes who hurried over to clear their places, pour their tea, or offer them preserves (or, on the other hand, when the airplane had brought them back from the heart of Asia and they were again at the shabby luxury hotel, the somnambulistic servants, shabby too, who disappeared for an hour or so: but they had picked up this habit themselves: wait—wait for departures, for meetings, for ceremonies), no longer were they surprised anymore at their hosts' prodigious capacity for making speeches, at the length of their speeches evoking in turn (as much as it was possible to grasp what was meant from the hesitant murmurings of the interpreters) the wisdom of the old shepherds, the legends of the genies of the mountain, and the sacred aura of the lake surrounded by the peaks of those mountains after which their convention had been emphatically named (they were taken there for a day by airplane—a little propeller-driven apparatus, the interior looked like a lounge: a lounge for businessmen or for billionaires, with a deep carpet, chairs covered with natural linen, with little ruffled curtains also of linen, framing the portholes through which one could see the terrifying summits gliding majestically below, turning slowly, showing their dizzying faces one after the other, their terrify-ing walls of ice, the sparkling solitudes, while inside the comfortable lounge the loud bursts of laughter erupted, unreal, punctuating the jokes of the film star Nero (a Russian-born- naturalized Englishman who lived in Switzerland: continuously, with no pause, talking, neither his voice nor his handsome face, a little fleshy like a Roman emperor's, betray-ing the slightest change, he emptied one of the glasses of vodka—not a shot glass: a glass—that the hostess offered them: with one gulp, replacing it on the tray before she had the time to turn toward any of the other guests, the sentence, the story begun (he had just returned from a trip to China, and was imitating, comically, the guttural voices of his hosts and the mistakes they made speaking English) continuing in the same tone, as though he had simply taken a breath or swallowed some saliva and not five ounces of 80-proof alcohol, caustic, Neronian, as superbly British—as only a Russian-born Englishman can be—as his wavy, silver, styled hair, his tailor-made shirt, his tie, his cuff links, and the suit he wore, cut from a material found only in London on Savile Row).

They (the fifteen guests) held their meetings (or rather were assembled, were seated, after which they waited) in deep armchairs set around in a horseshoe shape at the head of which sat the burly gentleman, with the meaty face of a mountain man and dense, scrubby hair cut short, who had greeted them that night at the airport. The first day he spoke at great length in a grave tone, solemnly and laboriously, his brow wrinkled, leaving a pause at the end of each of his sentences to allow the interpreters a chance to translate, turning, one after the other, the pages of his speech or weaving in memories of his youth, the adages of the old folk of the mountains, invocations of the Egyptian pyramids, or Dostoyevski's novels, the marvels of Venice, or Shakespeare, and his wishes for world peace at the dawn of the twenty-first century. Then he was still, leaning back now in his armchair, his legs stretched out in front of him and crossed at the ankles, one elbow on the armrest, his hand supporting his massive head, as though offended, outraged, listening to the

applause that crackled to life even before the voices of the
interpreters finishing the last sentence had died out, rising to
dominate the piercing, obstinate applause, until it all stopped,
the sound of the torrent thrown back in echoes by the flanks
of the valley seeming to flow in again, to fill the silence with
its patient and eternal rushing.

And they (the fifteen guests) got used to that as well. That
is to say, to not hearing the female voices, dejected, dogged,
of the interpreters seated behind their deep armchairs, leaning over their shoulders, murmuring in their ears the endless
chain of words devoid of all sense, stumbling, making apol-
ogies, beginning again, while they looked out of the open
windows watching the rustling leaves of the poplars in the
sun, the poplars being stripped day after day by the autumn,
pale green, then yellow, gold, loosening, falling gently,
turning in the calm air or carried by a sudden breeze slanting
down sometimes, hundreds of them like a fall of snow. Sometimes one or another of them leaned toward his neighbor
across the large armrests, opening a conversation in lowered
voices, the two heads drawn close—or taking notes—or
pretending to, writing a letter, signing postcards—then
drawing back into his armchair, silent, his eyes following for
the hundredth time the design of the fake Persian carpet.

For one whole hour, one evening (it was night, but as it was
warm in the room one of them asked to have a window
opened, and again the silvered rushing of the torrent,
majestic, indifferent, came to them), they listened to one of
their hosts speak, breathless, hurried, almost choking (Nero,
dressed by the tailors of Savile Row, maintained that if they
spoke so much it was to justify the expenditure made—for,
divided by the greatest number of words possible, the price

1

Claude Simon

of each one of them would be established at a level acceptable to their accounting department), suggesting to the fifteen guests that they inscribe their names on the crystal cubes with which a pyramid would be built, that they engrave the peaks of the mountain and construct a palace where all the peoples of the world could meet. They heard the painter who was decorated like a general (to tell the truth, except for grand occasions—receptions or photographic sessions—he had traded in his breathtaking uniform for grey flannel trousers and an elegant checkered jacket bought, without a doubt, in the same place where he had been taught both to speak and to paint in English), he too was gifted, with an inexhaustible capacity for speaking, lyrical, rolling his eyes in his bronze head, verbose, easily linking sentence after sentence, with his pure Oxford accent, his gladiator's features slightly fleshy, childlike, tireless, while the man with the head of a mountain man shifted about in his presidential armchair, leaning his heavy head first on his left fist, then on his right, then leaning back, his neck pressed against the high back of the chair, his eyes on the ceiling, his legs again stretched out in front of him, ankles crossed, his hands folded on his stomach, then, as though suddenly awakened, sitting up again, turning to the left, making a sign with his hand, his index finger lifted (as one snaps his fingers to get the attention of a waiter or a servant), the chief interpreter hurrying over, the president (now turned completely to the side, his left arm hung over the back of the chair, his left side against the back, one leg folded underneath him, turning his back on the gladiator who was still speaking) talking in a low voice to him (the chief interpreter: a round, jovial, affable man with the face of a headwaiter or a police commissioner) and he, straightening up, walking around the circle of armchairs, behind them, silently, on tiptoe, to the place occupied by the Mediterranean diplomat, bending to his ear, speaking to him, the diplomat acquiescing with a nod of his head, standing, coming around his own chair and then following the chief interpreter and walking like him, on tiptoe, passing in the opposite direction the circle of armchairs until reaching the president's chair, sitting, at the president's invitation, in one of the smaller chairs that had been placed slightly back from the circle, pulling himself closer, the president, the chief interpreter, bent over double, and the diplomat discussed, all three, in lowered voices (and once the gladiator seemed to notice something, hesitated, cast a glance at the three men, seemed on the point of stopping, slowing down, his voice weakening, but, with a quick movement of his chin, the diplomat drew the president's attention to him, the president turning toward the gladiator, nodded his head and gestured vigorously in a sign of approbation and of encouragement, and turned back to his discussion) a sheet of paper now in his hand, the chief interpreter translating for him a text that the diplomat had also taken out of his pocket, the heavy head of the mountain man with eyes half closed nodding gently up and down, then, suddenly raising a hand, interrupting the chief interpreter, holding out to him while tapping with his bent index finger the page that he held and indicating that he should translate it to the diplomat, applause suddenly broke out, the gladiator gathering his notes, nodding his thanks, smiling, confused, his eyes like those that one sees in paintings representing people in ecstasy in religious paintings, raised up to heaven, showing their whites, the president turning quickly in his armchair, also applauding, the diplomat stuffing the paper between his legs to applaud, the photographer's flashbulbs popping one after the other, the president checking the time on his watch and waiting for the excitement to die down to propose a pause before hearing the next orator.

They were photographed outside as well, a bit dazzled, blinking in the sunlight, in front of the building with the name translated from the Chinese inscribed in letters of gold across the edifice. They were photographed with spade and watering can in hand, as they each pretended to be planting a symbolic tree at the foot of which lay a plaque bearing his name, on the lawn that stretched in front of the city library (the city—that is to say, not an agglomeration developed slowly through the ages, through successive periods of growth, around the cross-roads of trade routes, a market, a citadel, a place of exchange or of prayer, with, at its center, narrow alleyways, a bazaar, the remains of ramparts, but something that had suddenly surged forth from nothingness or from a past—a caravansary, mosque, fortress, or broken-down cottages—bulldozed to erect in their place what the architects certified by the school of architecture and the urban development specialists certified by the school of urban development call a city nowadays, like any of those that spring up about every twenty-four hours on the surface of the earth, and this one neither more nor less ugly, not more nor less absurd than Lagos, Mexico, or those in the province of Val-de-Marne, with the one difference that, in this case, the computer seemed to have been programmed to turn out the colossal and pompous: something already dead before being born, prefabricated in haste (cement, columns, marble facing, and trees all included) by some specially con-ceived giant machine, some electronic brain mechanically distributing (as on those little luminous screens on which

hasty outlines appear, flashing jerkily, and organize themselves one after the other into a concise, general image)
living quarters, uninhabitable quarters but inhabited all the
same, administration quarters, business districts, visitors'
quarters, all encircling an opera, a library (lacking books), an
auditorium, a museum (lacking exhibits), a House of Congress
or a Hall of the People, all flanked by a stadium and an airport
according to the local topography: the airport at which they
had arrived, from which they could see, lifting off like wasps,
when they were brought back during the day, combat helicopters painted a somber green or grey).

They were brought here sometimes (to the city), on the
occasion of ceremonies of the same type as the tree-planting
or their audiences, and they could see again the colossal
avenues, three-quarters empty, with intersections at which
the brown uniformed militiamen held up the rare automobile
or two and the crammed buses dragging their bellies and trail-
ing their plumes of black smoke, the nagging red cheesecloth
banners with the incomprehensible injunctions displayed in
the parks and at intersections, the paradoxical orgy of archi-
tectures of cement and of marble erected within the limits of
the steppe, emphatic, constructed, it seemed, for the single
purpose of appearing in the color photographs of tourist
brochures side by side with those of women picking cotton,
the creations of the local artisans and the arc welders.

The houses in which they were lodged were distributed
throughout a park of about one hundred acres, five kilometers
from the city, planted with fruit trees and poplars, surrounded
on all sides by impassable grillwork which one could leave
only through a gate guarded by a police substation in front of
which the lead car in the cortege stopped, waiting for a

militiaman, he too in khaki, to come out (a noncommissioned officer no doubt—or a corporal—wearing a holster at his side), who approached buttoning up his tunic, examined the papers the chauffeur handed to him, or pretending to examine them: like a rite, an obligatory formality (the same as the long discussion that he had with the chief interpreter each time—as though it were indispensable that he have some papers, a discussion, a wait—perhaps simply to justify his function, to obey some secret custom: through the wide-open window of the guardhouse one could see an absolutely blank wall, painted that yellow that the warrant officers and colonels of all the barracks all over the world have such affection for, and one electric light bulb, also naked, hanging at the end of its cord; a militiaman inside the station noticed that the passenger in the lead car was looking inside: he switched off the light): a rite, thus a ceremony, the face of the noncommissioned officer perfectly inexpressive, his eyes inexpressive (neither inquisitive nor vigilant, not even interested: inexpressive) while the cortege of automobiles, counted and recounted, finally moved off and he (the officer) watched them passing now with their share of occupants similar to the guests of some wedding, including the couple, the two black pastors seated parallel to each other on the rear seat, solemn, imperturbable, wrapped to their chins in their severe turtleneck sweaters, their somber ebony visages thrown back, like two ambassadors, two bishops of some congregation or of some African diocese on their way to some ecumenical council in a chauffeured limousine: they (the fifteen guests) were received by the municipal council, that is to say, about twenty large, round, yellow faces with slanting eyes, strangled by their neckties, atop stiff suits, presided over by the mayor (a European, still young, slender, discreetly elegant, with an unpronounceable and supranational name such that it (the name) allowed its bearer to fit in whether holding the office of first magistrate of a Central Asian city of a million inhabitants or as an advisor to the president of the United States or deputy of a French province with a reactionary majority), and they had to hear the speeches again, step forward, each at the call of his name, to have draped over their shoulder a velvet sash on which was embroidered in gold letters and in the two languages written in Cyrillic characters their standing as honorary citizens: always preceded by the troop of photographers walking backwards and flashing, they had also to visit the library in front of which they had pretended to plant the young trees, mount the solemn staircase, seat themselves around tables on which dishes of fruit and doughnuts were spread, drink cups of tea, shake hands, smile. The mayor gave a banquet, and during the speeches they exchanged and compared their porcelain plates on which couples of women tenderly intertwined were pictured, dressed in the classical style, tunics, mauve, or the green of the Nile, and around them flew cupids with transparent wings like a dragonfly's, shooting arrows from golden bows (the settings, glasses, and the porcelain service with the suggestive embraces seized without a doubt by decree from some sybarite prince or count of the previous century, now mass-produced, also by decree, by some huge manufacturing company—or by a department of the gigantic, and unique, factory that produced the line of cities conceived by the computer, columns, frescoes, statues, table settings— coffee cups and sugar bowls included—delivered by whole trains, throughout all the republics of the Union, even the most isolated, in the middle of deserts, of forests where the ground never thaws, at the foot of fabulous mountain ranges, and placed by quiet, diligent servants (it was warm in the banquet room and they had to open a window here too—but, in the city, one did not hear the torrent) at the places of the municipal councillors, the distant descendants, civilized (or tamed) of Genghis Khan, flat, round, yellow faces covered by a fixed smile, impassable, impenetrable, as impassable as a papier-mâché mask, crowning their ties and their stiff suits, they too made of some cardboardlike material).

And during all this time (except during the banquets when they (the interpreters) were eating at the foot of the table, which meant that they (the guests) could at last dispense with the pretense of listening to them, having nothing to do but to wait staring at their plates during the interminable exchange of welcomes, and thanks, and wishes for peace among all people; and once (this happened later, when they were returning to the capital and they were taken to visit a monastery on the outskirts of town—and the same cortege of black automobiles speeding along, and the same militiamen in brown uniforms held up the traffic at each intersection: the woods, the forests having lost the last of their leaves, naked in the autumn sun (the sun already low on the horizon, dallying, in that interval of neutrality when, before burying themselves under the snow for months, curling up in the iron sheet of ice that would grasp and hold them, the silvered trunks of the birches seemed to want to profit from this last respite to sparkle one last time in the sunlight against the carpet of dead leaves), so, once (and yet another banquet, more speeches or rather an interminable dialogue, an inter- minable tête-à-tête where the only ones who took part (to

The Invitation

confront each other), in their incomprehensible language, in
turn silky, sibilant and animated, were their host (the man
with the massive head of a mountain man) and a monk
(priest, bishop, or recluse?) with a black beard, both gifted
with that fabled—orgiastic, so to speak—capacity for discussion, both listening to each other patiently, waiting, each
responding to a river of words with a river of his own, the
American (he was not only the second husband of the most
beautiful girl in the world, but had also written some successful plays dealing with successful subjects like, for example,
the suicide—some said: assassination by the secret police—
of that soft-shouldered living doll with breasts like ripe fruit
and a husky, baby voice) searching, then pulling a small note-
book from his pocket, tearing out a page, scribbling quickly
with a pencil, then, impassive, his dry, gaunt, inexpressive
expression, sliding the sheet across the tablecloth brushing
his neighbor's elbow (the neighbor drawn out of his somno-
lence, shifting stiffly in his chair, looking down, able to read,
on the small rectangle of paper, the words: "They find us contemptible") ... so, during all this time (while they visited the
library, planted trees, nibbled the fruits, out of politeness, that
were placed in front of them, drank innumerable cups of tea,
received medals), during all this time, the plaintive, exhausted, and tenacious voices of the interpreters followed
them, badgering, translating, monotone, the emphatic
speeches, reciting the timetable for the next day, pathetic in
their obstinacy, their goodwill, their conviction and their
simple language like the language one uses when talking to
idiots, four-year-old children, or animals, until evening,
finally, come back to their gaudy apartments, finally alone,
they could sit still for a moment, exhausted themselves, then

standing, opening the windows on the monumental night, stepping out onto the terrace and standing, breathing the still air, listening to the peaceful sound of the furious torrent, the whispering of the last leaves on the poplars invisible in the night: quiet rustlings, murmurings, silence.

. . . and now he (the secretary-general—or rather the interpreters seated in the little cubicles along the wall parallel to the long table: it was now no longer women that they heard, their unhappy voices tired, stumbling: but men now, whom each of the guests, headphones over his ears, could hear in his own language, the sure tones following the assured speech of the secretary-general speaking without looking at any one of them in particular (none of the fifteen seated guests, seven on one side, eight on the other, here and there at the table on which the only element of luxury was the bottles of mineral water: the fifteen guests whom his counselors had said (or whom his counselors had been told) were, each in his own country, important men (or bought out already—or complacent—or sensitive to flattery) and whom he (the secretary-general) took for nothing more than that, though he judged it wise (which his counselors had judged wise) to spend (to have him spend) two hours of his time (he who did not have much to spare, could not only destroy half the world but still order a corporal to put out the lights in a police station where there was nothing more to see than a yellow wall and to send helicopters armed with machine guns to shoot down mountain tribesmen armed only with flintlocks) with people whose only capacity was to write books, to act in movies, to paint portraits in the English style, or to draft economic treaties (and probably his own experience of economic problems made him see these as less important than the others—except to take into account their influence not on the laws of the markets but proportionally to their renown): nevertheless he didn't have the choice and he had to make do with what he had, methodist pastors and gladiator included, doubtlessly weighing them while he spoke, that is to say, evaluating, estimating that immaterial, subtle, and poisonous something that radiates from an audience, that he must break down with fifteen people the same as with a crowd, not drawing on what he learned (could have learned) at the college in Vaud, in which he never once set foot, but on the wisdom that he was able to acquire on this subject in the course of an existence (an ascension) that was also subtle, that is to say, in the case which occupied him at the moment, that intuitive knowledge (the wisdom) of the prejudices, favorable or not, that could be held regarding him by the fifteen guests prepared for a week now by caviar, smoked tongue, and salmon (not to mention a bishop and a prima ballerina) for the privilege of finding themselves seated at a table at the head of which one of the two most powerful men in the world now sat, and spoke to them, affably; great honor, for which the client of the Savile Row tailor had not hesitated, risking fatigue (though it is true, missing the audience with the bishop and the old dancer—but he had no doubt seen others) to fly nonstop from the heart of Central Asia all the way to his adopted country or rather the country (the hospitable Helvetic Confederacy) in which he, for reasons of personal convenience, resided and had several urgent business matters to put into order, then, taking again to the air,

returned (all in forty-eight hours and at this moment) seated
with the fourteen other guests at the table provisioned only
with mineral water: thus the secretary-general now faced, in
his attempt at reeducation, a burlesque sampling of professions and races selected by his counselors (there was also an
Indian, soberly dressed, however, in European fashion—as
for the yellow race, the Tolstoy of Central Asia who followed
his host in the capital had served him, if not perhaps as a
representative at least as an intermediary), and (since he had
already four days before displayed his formidable arsenal at
the poker table on the other side of which the cowboy with
the flashy smile sat also with a formidable arsenal—each
carefully guarding the ace in the hole that, in the manner of
cardsharps everywhere, they kept up their sleeves—never
forgetting the two revolvers negligently pointed under the
green felt table in the direction of their respective stomachs)
with no other weapon now than his personal charisma aug-
mented by his prestige as secretary-general: and no doubt he
perceived that (that is to say, that mixture of flattered vanity,
of consideration if not of admiration, of curiosity if not of
confidence, of expectation if not of agreement) the same as
he had had to notice, on each step of his way to the top, the
contradictory unions of ambition and laziness, of cowardice
and courage, or treachery and fidelity, stupidity and trickery
on which he had played, betting alternately, double or nothing,
on one or on the other, having reached now that position
which, under cover of the obligatory vocabulary of convention
and quotes from supporting texts, permitted him to indulge
in a veritable refutation, announcing, in his affable, measured
tones, sentences which, thirty years earlier, would have been
rewarded, trial or not, with an expedient bullet in the neck

and, just two years ago, with a sentence of living death in some frozen desert, or, at best, commitment to an insane asylum, with the appearance at this moment of someone who, having succeeded by elbowing his way through to push himself to the front of a crowd, had suddenly seen something which had made him stop dead in his tracks, his arms protectively raised, in the posture of a man with his back up against the base of some wall that was cracking open, trying, if not to stop, at least to slow, to contain, to turn the formidable pressure of the moving mass (if ever movement could be called the action of staying still in the midst of general movement) driven by inertia alone, a few of those in the front of the crowd perhaps followed his example while those who came after continued, amorphous and somnambulistic, to bunch together, to close in, to pile up, so that it was not only the fully loaded revolver of the retired cowboy that was aimed at his stomach but still another, just as fully loaded, pressed against his loins, which he said, moreover, not in these terms of course, to his fifteen guests, but using (always with that equivocal mixture of honesty and duplicity typical of politicians) the same vocabulary of convention lacking still that emphasis which seemed for his countrymen . . .

AND all during two long hours in the refectory of the monastery—or at least the room in which the table was set for the dinner that the bishop offered—or at least the dinner that the bishop had accepted—or had been obliged to accept—that it should be held in the monastery and that he should preside over it (bishop and monastery were included with the sacred lake of the mountains, the celebrated prima ballerina, and the crown jewels in the attractions selected for the fifteen guests as though (except for the lake—even if the occult powers attributed to it by old legends could win for it consideration as a legacy bequeathed by the past . . .) their hosts had believed that they could provide nothing better for their distraction—or their edification—than to draw from their reserves of antiquities (folklore, old ballerina, old diamonds as big as walnuts—even if someone (the American?) said, in an aside, that they were false, that the real ones had all been sold sixty years ago on the markets in London and Amsterdam to buy the wheat destined for the starving population: the only piece of gold plate to which one could accord any authenticity (in the cellar with steel doors, with guards armed with daggers, where they were obliged to stay for more than an hour to contemplate behind windows of armored glass the crowns, the heavy necklaces and the diadems sparkling with the iridescent fire of a glacier) consisted of a map of the Union a good meter and a half long and entirely made of collected diamonds, the immense and massive territory with the ragged coastline, the immense block of the steppes, of deserts frozen or boiling and of colossal mountains thanks to these last colonies on half of Europe and with the old covering almost half of Asia, which would have even encroached on the American continent if a greedy emperor had not sold that part (just as one would sell a stony field, a grassless prairie, or an infertile plot to a naïve neighbor, who was in this case—or was going to be—a successful consortium on Wall Street), twinkling like an ice floe, an ice floe that, in winter, was going to weld together, to enclose, in its bays, its crevasses, embracing as in a vise its capes and islands, as though the fantastic stretch of earth covered with diamonds glued together was entirely subject to (immobilized, over-laid, fixed by) a formidable phenomenon of glacial freezing preserving intact—if not edible—the bodies of gigantic mammoths, of gigantic human or animal species (like the seminarian) made to disappear and preserved by the cold for the future edification of paleontologists, school children, and the curious) . . . so, the room (not the monk's refectory: a room with walls paneled with pine to the height of a man, then bare, painted with a neutral colored enamel, only decorated by an icon with a gold base, with a color reproduction of da Vinci's *Last Supper* and of a sticky painting in oil representing a blond, downy Christ drawing open his acid blue tunic to point out on his acid red shirt a heart of burning gold) exhaling that indefinable odor of mustiness and of rancid flesh, special to the celibate, that in all latitudes seems to stagnate in those places where any community of humans joins to live in continence and prayer, impregnating even the walls themselves (men wearing robes, like women, their long black dresses also exhaling from their folds something both gloomy, cadaverous, and vaguely carnivalesque, like disguises, the proud, the haughty and ostentatious external manifestation of that morgue particular to prophets, to men of God and to eunuchs—even if the servants: not young novices as one would expect here, but five or six of those creatures, them-selves asexual, ageless, stout and masculine, like little bundles, coming and going with their fat faces in the silence rustling their starched aprons hiding their fat thighs, their fat vulvas consecrated to an eternal, sanctimonious and sour virginity); and these: above the discreet rattle of knives and

51

forks, the two voices (one, that of the bishop—the prophet?—: a personage who was still young, fifty at most, full cheeked, with a black forked beard, with abundant black hair tied up into a bun, and the other, that of Tolstoy come by airplane from Central Asia) alternating, answering each other, both calm but both demonstrating the same impassioned vehemence, controlled; and not a dialogue, the replies more or less long or more or less brief, but, in the tongue like honey mixed with colored crayons, debating or rather disputing, each waiting patiently until the other had finished before speaking (or rather, to begin an oration in his turn), the man of God with eyes flashing under thick black Jupiterian eyebrows, severe, imperturbable, barely turning his head toward the other as he spoke, then continuing, his eyes fixed beyond his plate—and then, not exactly speaking the wailings or the stammerings of History but its mutterings: something like what one can see in antique miniatures, the margins ornamented with interlacing leaves: two daises with bishops sitting across from, facing each other wearing their miters, assembled in some basilica in Asia Minor or Germany to dispute some schism, some fundamental article of dogma, or the deposition of a pope: no longer the world that they (the fifteen guests, forgotten, ignored, seated, tormented by cramps, on their chairs) had left outside getting out of the fifteen automobiles that had carted them with all speed through the forests of birches finishing the casting off of their leaves just until the appearance of the wall above, which shimmered like sparkling gold with dozens of turrets and pinnacles outlined by the hazy sky—still hearing the bishop and his companion pursuing the exchange, of liturgical responses, so to speak, this recitative for two voices—like a ceremonial, a rite stripped of sense but scrupulously observed: the American again leaning over, taking back the little rectangle of paper on which he had written earlier "They find us contemptible," scribbling quickly on the back: "Just think: this is an *informal* meeting!" and pushing it again toward his neighbor's napkin, the word *informal* underlined two times, the bottom line an exasperated scrawl, infuriated, tearing the edge of the thin slip of paper, speaking at the same time out of the corner of his mouth, saying: "Yes: informal. As you can see," without turning his head, impassive, shifting his ossifying limbs, fidgeting in his chair, crossing and recrossing his legs, then again immobile, his wooden expression showing nothing, his right elbow in his left hand, his right hand pinching the tip of his nose in a gesture typical to him—"Yeah?" he said later. "Yeah! . . ." (the fifteen guests now walking, stretching their stiff legs on the stones of the court between the churches—some (the eldest) simply whitewashed, others with walls and porches ornamented with luxurious cornices, capitals, columns with curling sculptured foliage, painted pink, green, almond, ocher—". . . really: you haven't seen the film? They made it themselves (not the monks, but a type of their official cinematography—which didn't keep it from being banned, then, nevertheless, they ended up giving them permission to show it): that all happened, I don't know when: when they started to build the first churches, I think: and the same fellows with beards, the same cantors that we heard this morning at that mass they took us to, and the ones that arrived at full gallop at the foot of I don't know which steppe, with the slanted eyes and black drooping mustaches, and who galloped into the churches, whipping the kneeling figures or riding them down, breaking the icons, gorging themselves on the Host

and the Holy Wine, tying one of the bearded ones by the
feet to a horse's tail and sending him dragging off . . . After
which, when they had gone, the others (I mean the bearded
ones) rebuilt their churches with still more gilt (because they
could make the muzhiks sick of gold, you know), painting
other icons, casting new bells and setting themselves again to
chanting . . ."

. . . the secretary-general continuing to explain to the two
black evangelists, to a general-painter, to a Nero of the cinema,
to a president of an economics society, to an American from
Hollywood, to an elegant diplomat, and to the other guests
that he could not relieve the pressure of the revolver pressed
against his loins except by first relieving to a certain extent
the pressure of the pistol that the retired cowboy held
directed at his stomach, hidden under the cloth of the
negotiating table—or the other way around: unimportant, it
came to the same in the last analysis . . .—or perhaps it was
only important to him to gain time, to contain the inert and
blind thrust against which he braced himself with all his
strength with his back and his arms spread wide—or only not
to stop talking during the time that he needed to exchange
his revolver for a more powerful one while he struggled to
protect that blind mass from that something that he had
suddenly seen, terrifying enough to cause him to dig in his
heels—but he was not a mule: so only two heels, his legs
propping him up, the soles of his elegant shoes impeccably
polished sliding in the mud, the mute, amorphous multitude
by the force of its inertia alone threatening every moment

to overrun him, to push him under, to pass over him, and to trample him without seeing him, just carried by its own weight, without hatred or malice, slowly but inexorably . . .

I t snowed. That was when the airplane had brought them back from the shores of the sacred lake. It snowed during the night on the lowest foothills of the mountain, on the trees of the orchards whose branches still covered with leaves bent to the ground under the weight of the snow that also clung like white hats to the large, gold letters of the Chinese name written in Cyrillic characters across the facade of the building in which they met: a first snow, fallen as though by accident, and which the still warm autumn sun melted in a morning, leaving pockets of white only here and there in shady hollows and, on cement courtyards, puddles of water.

It had not snowed (though it was two thousand meters higher) on the shores of the lake: a lake itself on the scale of the rest of the landscape, the monstrous mountains, the monstrous steppe and the monstrous climate (one of the interpreters said that in the plain the temperature reached one hundred degrees to fall sometimes in winter to minus one hundred . . .), big (the lake), four or five times the size of Lake Geneva, like a small inland sea where from time to time sudden tempests would break loose with terrible howling winds from the summits, after which the lake would become incredibly calm again, spreading its solid blue surface reflecting the sunlight, enveloped by the mountains of ice on all sides. There was a private beach with slides, beach cabins, diving board, and fine sand, light brown in color, reserved for the guests of . . . (but what to call it?: again a park surrounded by impassable grillwork and with residences scattered over it a little less vast but just as sumptuous as those that they had just left, furnished also from a color catalog (mahogany, oriental carpets, baskets of fruit wrapped in cellophane, gleaming bathrooms), grouped around a conference chamber (so that they could hear, one more time, the painter-general: apparently the English he had been taught permitted him not only to paint in that language but also to speak inexhaustibly on any subject at all) where they found the inevitable interpreters, more exhausted than ever (they had been brought in not by air but by bus, over terrible mountain roads): "Can you imagine having it this good anywhere else?" said the caustic Savile Row client as he took a short stroll with two of the other guests: "Tranquil, eh?" He pretended to look around distrustfully: "Something beyond doubt like what they call a rest home, no? A . . ." Suddenly he grabbed his companion's arm, pulling him hard, clinging to him as though in panic: "Hey! look at those two over there . . ." (two women—or rather two giants—dressed entirely in white, with little white caps like surgeons or nurses, white stockings, white shoes, standing in an alleyway watching them): "Hey! they look like thugs! What the . . . Hey! Watch out! Act natural. Don't make any sudden moves! . . . In this country one never knows . . . They're very lenient with the insane, you know? . . ." still playing the buffoon (all that was missing were the toga, the lyre, Rome in flames, and the golden crown of oak leaves resting on the silver locks tumbling down on his neck, like those of a member of the House of Lords or the champion of a regatta), the two cleaning

women noticing that they had been seen disappeared quickly
(just as the corporal had doused the light in the police station)
as if frightened, caught in the act, behind a hedge, with their
aprons and their buckets, the park in the tepid autumnal air
paradoxically less denuded by the fall than the park that they
had left two thousand meters below, just touched with gold,
making one think of the park of some•deserted casino, of
health spas where, out of season, important diplomats or the
plenipotentiaries of countries at war with one another met in
secret away from prying eyes—or simply their families on
vacation and whose children play on the slides, hide in the
beach cabins, and dive into the water from the heights of the
diving board under the protection of the solid enclosing grillwork: there was also (same whitewashed cottages, same grey-
green roofs of slate or tile, same gardens where the last flowers
bloomed) a village that the bus had passed coming to the little
airport and where one of the guests asked if he could go to
take some photos, the interpreter saying: "Of course! . . ."
saying: "I shall go find out . . ." saying: "Wait for me, I'll give
you a tour, I will go ask for a car . . ." disappearing, returning
after a long moment, saying: "Right away, we're going!" then
disappearing again, a long moment passes again, the interpreter reappearing finally, saying: "What a pity! It's time for
lunch. Everyone is already seated! I looked all over for you . . ."
or "Unfortunately they are expecting us at the party. You will
see. It is very nice. It will be fun. You can take photos! . . ."; the
party: two or three hundred men's faces, round and flat, with
slanting eyes, smooth or covered with wrinkles, weathered
closer to copper (or leather) than yellow, like the faces of
those indefatigable mountaineers, those sherpas one sees in
photographs of Himalayan expeditions, capable of climbing

up vertical mountainsides, loaded down like mules, a strap around their foreheads, wearing here little hats just like Tyrolean hats except made of white felt, with black lining, all turning at once to watch the fifteen guests seat themselves above them in the places of honor, their hands encumbered with flowers, applauding those who came up toward them from out of the crowd of spectators with the little caps, seating themselves, setting the cumbrous flowers down wherever they could, and opening the program which announced a horse show, wrestling, races; the sky grew slowly overcast: a blanket of clouds like a veil, higher than the highest of the mountains, vaporous, flat, immobile.

... the secretary-general's affable voice turning lightly ironic for a moment, caustic, his face smiling with malice, to say to his fifteen guests that according to what he had been told they had talked a great deal during the past week but had worked little, the two methodist pastors (to tell the truth, it had been learned that one of them was an actor, a star in Harlem) laughing suddenly, bursting out with that bizarre laughter, uncontrolled, wild, sharp, like a horse's whinny, the secretary-general speaking all the while looked over at them, his smile broadening, either because he shared their fun, or because he was amused by their boisterous hilarity, then no longer looking at them, continuing, the laughing stopped ...

The Invitation

Through the open door at the center of the iconostasis one could see the backs of three officiating priests dressed in ample gold chasubles, making large, slow gestures, standing immobile sometimes (concentrated, absorbed in some essential prayer, some meditation?), then in motion again majestically, the iconostasis itself resplendent with gold, a broad beam of sunlight penetrating through the window, to the right, causing sparkling reflections to spring up out of the shadows, a pope dressed in black standing on the right in front of his pulpit, raising and replacing again and again according to the stages of his office the high, cylindrical headdress, black also, the fifteen guests standing in the front row among the crowd of the faithful—the young and the old —kneeling or prostrating themselves in turn, their foreheads against the tiles like Moslems and, on the left, in a sort of elevated enclosure, the choir of young monks with profound deep voices, the curious child raising his head, the old woman beside him angrily pushing it back down, his forehead thumping against the tiles, the name of the monastery itself like a dark gold flash streaking through the darkness: Zagorsk.

Elegant and rapid graceful-necked horses of that formerly wild breed that Tolstoy said were raced by dashing officers, young counts, and princes for a prize of gold (now the high ceiling of clouds thickened, hastening the dusk: only a saffron band, a little pink toward the bottom, separated the flat, immobile lid supported like an

awning by the chain of darkening, snowy peaks), each of the
graceful, delicate-limbed mounts, with swanlike necks, led
by the halter by the groom trotting at their sides, halting them
standing in profile, looking like an English engraving, in the
center of the ocher carpet spread on the ground in front of
the tribune across which critical murmurs rippled, certain of
the more nervous beasts bucking the empty air, rearing up,
the groom lifted off the ground, suspended on the halter, the
admiring murmurs growing—then, on the same ocher carpet
wrestlers wearing baggy pantaloons, naked, muscular torsos
despite the chill coming on, their skin also coppery, bending
forward until horizontal, heads touching, the goal apparently
to hurl your opponent to the ground, toppling him with an
expert twist of the hips, allowed to hold him only by the belt.
Belts pink or pale green. Other subtle rules no doubt, the
combat interrupted constantly by the judge bent double himself, attentive, punctilious.

... the secretary-general, signifying the end of the discussion,
raising his voice slightly, endeavoring to sound persuasive (or
perhaps without having to try: perhaps persuaded himself,
after all...), then inclining his head, bending forward to push
back his chair, the fifteen guests standing all at the same time
with a scraping of chairs pushed back, the secretary-general
now standing, a gesture to thank his guests for their attention,
holding his hands with his palms vertical and parallel as
though he pressed between them two sides of a box, moving
his hands up and down slightly, his face cordial, then turning
to the side to speak for a moment with the elegant diplomat

and the Central Asian Tolstoy in a light babble of voices, the interpreters coming out of their cubicles, they too coming to converse for a moment with the guests, stepping aside to let the secretary-general pass by, skirting the table on the side with the cubicles, then stopping as does the master of the house near the door: it was finished, each of the guests shaking in passing his outstretched hand, hearing a few words in that language like a bird's feathery tail, at the same time wild, caressing, and colorful, then leaving.

the evening darkening, the light declining more and more, the band that separated the ceiling of clouds from the chain of icy peaks now saffron colored, the jockeys' hats not gaudily colored silk but cotton, without a doubt pastel colored, pale yellow, light rose, musty green, black, periwinkle blue, the whole countryside pastel but subdued (that is to say, like those pastels in chalk on a cardboard box, the cardboard showing through the stripes of color, blending the range of colors into variations of somber tones with only here and there a touch of acid, the lustrous cloth draped over the horses themselves like variations of auburn more or less somber or more or less pale, only the lake (the crowning stroke of the giant mountains now deep blue, heavy, almost black) like a metal plaque, glowing as though illuminated from below, as though returning all the light that it had soaked up during the day, green with streaks of rose, the horses setting off at the sound of the bell at full gallop, without strategy, whipped by the jockeys, and already twenty lengths between the first and the second at the first turn, and fifty by the next straightaway, the yellow cap on his head, a speck gliding along horizontally there in the dusk, the second with a cerise cap already beaten, the others straggling far behind, the night almost fallen now, the lake like yellow silver with pale traces of azure . . .

flowers, armfuls of carnations, gladiolus that young girls put into their hands, children with red scarves around their necks, with flat, yellow faces, with black hair, sleek and shining, and from whom they (the guests) tried to extricate themselves, bouquets even at their departure in the airplane that would take them back to the capital, placed hurriedly on the carpeting, tipped over, stems broken, already wilting, strewn along the central corridor, trampled by the comings and goings from one armchair to another, papers in hand, stooping to compare, hastily correct, words scratched out or scribbled in, grandiloquent sentences, empty of meaning, paragraphs empty of meaning, corpses of crushed flowers scattered over the carpet, ponds, blind lakes here and there covered with a white film already frozen in the expanse the color of a tawny beast, dotted with round clouds strung out parallel, followed by their shadows, the steppe too empty

silvered statue of a little bald man with a goatee, imperious, a tired man, sparkling in the sun, tiny against the backdrop of the shining mountains, photographed on the sly from the bus bouncing down the rutted roadway, anachronistic, blurred,

The Invitation

in a square amidst whitewashed cottages, grey roofs, also
blurred, slipping away horizontally

the fifteen guests standing on their reflections inverted in
the parquet mirror of expensively inlaid wood, colossal
chamber of Saint George, orgy of marble, of gold, benches
orange and black between the polished columns beneath the
windows, above which hung plaques with the names of royal
generals, princes, counts, grand dukes engraved in gold
letters, conquerors of Tartars, Swedes, Turks, Poles, Lithu-
anians, Ukrainians, French, Mongols, Prussians, Cross of
Saint George: Potëmkin, Suvorov, Bagration, Iermolov,
Kutuzov, Benningsen, Tomassov . . .

so old, ghostly, a ruin at the center of an empty plateau, dusty,
she too as though crumbling into dust, greyish, standing there
exhausted, large charcoal circles around her eyes, welcoming
the compliments with a smile, confused, harassed, thankful,
holding, in the crook of her arm, one of the bouquets, the
flowers already faded.

Having arrived in front of the mausoleum they stopped with a clicking of heels and, pivoting a quarter turn to the left, faced him, the underofficer between the two guards and a little behind, the five men (the two mounting guard, the two standing at each side of the entrance, waiting to be relieved, and the underofficer) perfectly immobile just until, without any order being given, the two soldiers mounting guard ascending the steps at a mechanical step, stopping, immobile for a time, then each effecting a quarter turn to come face-to-face with each of the two sentinels still frozen who, when the clock over the gate of the Savior finished counting out four strokes, made the butt of their rifles spring into their left hands, hip high, also effecting a quarter turn, now their backs to the mausoleum, starting down the steps with the same robotic step at the same time as their replacements advancing two steps, turning their backs effecting simultaneously a half turn, now face-to-face on either side of the entrance, letting their rifles drop, the butts smacking the marble slabs at the same time, the sound of the two impacts mingling, and coming to stand immobile.

The two men of the descending guard enclosing at present the underofficer, all three pivoting with the same movement to the left, always without any order being given, the guard on the right then throwing his leg stiffly out in front, passing between the underofficer and the mausoleum, coming the same level as the other guard who threw his leg forward in the same fashion, the underofficer falling into step with them, the three men now welded together, the studded boots hammering the marble paving stones, the right arms balancing the cadence of the step, the white-gloved hands thrown far

back behind, then swinging forward to the height of the butt
of the rifle, then backwards again, the rifle vertical balanced
in the left hand, backs straight, bayonets sparkling in the sun
as they skirted the high, red brick wall with the battlements
silhouetted by the wings of pigeons, passing in front of the
empty stands, the little pines planted in groups of three along
the rampart where under the rows of marble plaques reposed,
lying parallel, the embalmed mummies of the former rabble-
rousers with professors' foreheads, with their hurriedly knotted ties, their eyes closed behind their pince-nez, their faces
finally serene, peaceful, their lips now and from now on
closed.

Afterword

Claude Simon once remarked that "the kind of pleasure, or rather of 'profit,' that [the general public] expects from a novel is either that of an escape—where one forgets oneself for a few hours to identify with an exemplary hero or heroine comparable to some archetype (either good or evil)—or that of a teaching, of a bearing of knowledge which would propose a solution to the problems with which it is preoccupied . . ."[1] *The Invitation* comes up short on both counts. Neither a novel in the so-called realist tradition that allows for the full identification of reader with character and circumstance, nor one in the moral or otherwise pedagogical vein that resolves whatever issues may be at hand for the reader, it is a fiction that provokes a certain discomfort by its refusal to satisfy in either domain.

Lois Oppenheim

This discomfort is compounded by the difficulty of situating either author or text within the framework of any literary canon. Although associated since the early fifties by publisher (Minuit) and purpose (the renovation or updating, as it were, of novelistic form) with those writers known as the *nouveaux romanciers,* Simon reveals nothing in his work of the spiritual inheritance to which others of this group have been linked and his narrative aesthetics resembles that of the others only in its privileging of writing in an empirical (as opposed to omniscient or determinist) mode. Moreover, the very notion of the New Novel as a movement is in itself misleading; differences too numerous to enumerate and too profound to explicate here distinguish its writers and point to a specificity of each that reveals the superficiality of any effort to link them beyond a few common concerns. Indeed, *The Invitation* is further proof of an individualism that frustrates those readers seeking to impose on the chaos of modernist and the decenteredness of postmodernist literature principles of taxonomy.

And what of the difficulty of interpretation? The reader of *The Invitation* is ill at ease before the openness of a narrative whose meaning is blatantly plural and unrelated to any final, consumable Whole. What is clear, however, is that a reading that focuses on reconstituting the actuality of the visit to the Soviet Union by the fifteen guests of a certain renown, a reading that looks to restructure the reality of the recent effort to rehabilitate the disorder of the contemporary world, succeeds not in diminishing the discomfort, but in falsifying the fiction by reducing it to something entirely outside it. For such a reading, in pursuit of the ideological criticism assumed to be the referential point of departure, merely leads—through

68

the symbolist game that consists in localizing within the fiction references to reality and unscrambling them—to closure.

To remain attentive to the openness of *The Invitation* is to approach the work neither as a medium for the transmission of information *about* the visit nor as a formalization *of* that experience. Rather, it is to perceive the power of Simon's language to destructure the world as we know it and to reconstitute it on another order. This of course entails marginalizing the social and psychological conventions and ethical and political convictions that both inform the text and contextualize the meaning that we, as readers, give it. It entails bracketing allegorical and analogical presuppositions about the literary use of language and substituting for a positivist view of language as a reflection of the "real" the notion that the creative imagination functions rather as a simultaneous undoing and reformation of reality.

It is this view of the power of language to constitute as opposed to imitate that allows the reader of *The Invitation* to take pleasure in his reading: To perceive the numerous suspensions operative within the work as a resistance to totalization, whether linguistic (semantic, syntactic, or paradigmatic) or narrative, is to delight in Simon's play with perception and the imaginary as the primary forces of artistic creation. This is to say that if the work's numerous ellipses, repetitions, parenthetical asides and so on disconcert the reader, it is that they impede the plenitude or fullness of meaning that is the requisite (realist) illusion of conventional fiction. And yet, it is precisely these interregna and interpositions that activate the reader's participation in the work, *and hence his pleasure*, for, irreducible as representational signs

Lois Oppenheim

and symbols to collective (cultural) and individual (personal) codes or correlatives whose deciphering might provide some semblance of semantic continuity (where in actuality there is little), they accentuate the fundamentally interrogative function of Simon's language: "something (the episode—what should one call it?: the drama, the Shakespearean scene, the murder, the execution? the boxing match? . . .) arising not even then from the stutterings of History" (30).

The semantic fragmentation opens the text onto the intersubjective horizon of dialogue to the degree that it questions the reader's own frames of reference and tests his own willingness to play, imaginatively, with reality. Though characteristic of all the author's work, it is especially in *The Invitation* that a profoundly rhythmic syntax (to whose musical and poetic effects the unorthodox punctuation and seemingly endless duration of Simon's sentences contribute) combines with the evocative (as fragmented) semantic charge to at times disrupt and at times divert the enunciative flow. This is a syntax nourished by a regressive imagery—a return to primordial and elemental paradigms—that functions well outside the arena of rational and symbolic thought. Indeed, both the telluric and aquatic leitmotivs—the "old and monstrous mountain" and the forever invisible, but nonetheless audible, torrent—are inscribed within the narrative topology as elemental forces that not only underscore the substantiality of nature before the urban contrivances of man, but converge with the spatial and political immensities of the Soviet Union to overwhelm all that is human. And History itself arises from an elementarity, not that of nature but of "the ancestral status of beasts" (29), so that an assassination reconstituted in fantasy is "something . . . arising not

70

even then from the stutterings of History, from its stammerings, but from its wailing—and not savage, barbarous, but precisely animal, that is to say, necessity not by calculation, ambition, but the simple and primitive instinct of preservation. . ." (30). Primordiality in Simon defeats the logic of representation, the rationale of symbolic or allegoric depiction, to effect in its stead, syntactically and paradigmatically, a tension between the transparency (or referentiality) and opacity (or self-reflexivity) of language.

The "pleasure" of *The Invitation* thus emanates from ruptures in the signifying systems of language, from mutations in the semantic, syntactic, and paradigmatic structures that, in ordinary discourse, both restrain or contain reference and induce meaning. The openings or gaps in signification, however—insofar as they derive from a disregard for the anecdotal, from a total disinterest on the part of the author in reportage—are determined by the suspension of a number of givens of narration that, traditionally, have defined the pleasures (or "profits": escape and teaching) of the novel (as *The Invitation* might well be called) genre. This is to say that, besides calling into question *linguistically* the relations of word to world (and thereby reopening a philosophic can of worms that, in the history of Western thought from Plato to Heidegger, has never remained closed for very long), *The Invitation* suspends *narratively* all that would justify a "guess-the-referent" reading.

The most evident of the narrative suspensions is that of "story": Just as any recourse on the part of the reader to non-fictive character prototypes negates the text qua text in denying the only true existence of the fictive guests, the *literary* one, it is the decomposition of the visit to the Soviet

71

Union (on the order of reality) and its recomposition (on the order of fiction) that constitutes the aesthetic achievement. And yet, the tension between referential and nonreferential writing, the play between allusion to reality (and "the stutterings of History") and its surpassing in invention and the imaginary, is never fully resolved in *The Invitation* for it is within a focus on *scene*—as opposed to narrated event—that Simon's creativity is set. Though activities (the ballet, the visit to the fourteenth-century monastery, and the numerous ceremonies and receptions attended by the guests) provide a framework suitable for a story line, the dissolution of narrative time (through the intermixing of tenses, the persistent return of the present participle, the repetitions and parenthetical intrusions) undoes at every turn the linearity required for its establishment.

This divestment of narrative content—for scenic vision is descriptive, not anecdotal—results from the suspension of both identity and affect as well as that of temporal cohesiveness. Through the absence of any clear indication of an individual's thinking or feeling (the "perhaps . . . or perhaps not" motif undoes whatever we think we may know of the guests at any given moment) and that of any substantial interaction between the travelers, the narration opens onto a sort of phantom universe ideal in its adaptability to the reader's ever-changing projections. From the start, existence precludes essence (to reformulate Sartre's dictum), the pronominal substituting for any form of nomination: "Ordinarily (that is to say, since their arrival in the country, ten days before) they were all driven. . ." (7). This irruption of anonymity at the center of the realistic edifice the reader expects to have constructed before him and the continued use of the pronoun, followed throughout the text by the parenthetical bracketing of "the fifteen guests," clearly exemplifies the Simonian practice of formalism within a contextualized arena. Individuation does, at times, counterbalance anonymity—either through brief (and often humorous) reference to the nonfictive: "a man who had attained this position not by virtue of any special capacities or knowledge but by galloping on a horse, wearing a cowboy hat and grinning from ear to ear, in B movies" (10), or through the lengthy (and often horrific) nonreferential association of images: "the tiny silhouette . . . like a phantom apparition whose glow, it seemed, could be coming as easily from its own luminous substance as from the light of the beam shining upon it: not flesh, muscles, and skin but formed, it seemed, of some phosphorescent material, its contours imprecise, blurred, nebulous. . ." (11). Never, however, do the individualizing particulars succeed in fixing characterization outside of the anonymity/individuation dialectic.

What are we to make of the status and identity of the narrator himself? At once participant and spectator, his ambiguous relation to the narration reveals the interplay of autobiography and fiction that is, on the one hand, the primary preoccupation of Simon in all his previous works and, on the other, what has come to define the kind of realism associated with the recent writings of the so-called New Novelists in general: No longer centered on the liberation of the novel from the referentiality of fiction to the quotidian world, on the exploration of the objective world through the fusion of subject and object in perception or on the reduction of that relation to the linguistic structures that shelter it, the "autofiction" of these writers (Alain Robbe-Grillet, Nathalie

Sarraute, Robert Pinget, Michel Butor, Marguerite Duras) is grounded now in another referential framework, a historical one, whose focus on the past points to the processes of fictionalization themselves: The objectivation of the past by a consciousness operative in the present and by the fixing of lived experience in language deforms and hence falsifies its actuality (thereby fictionalizing it) to both muddle the distinction between biography and fiction and to confuse the relation of the narrator to his discourse.

In *The Invitation*, the ambiguity of the relation of narrator to narration reflects, in addition, the tension between the constructivism, or refusal to ascribe to writing ontological or epistemological truths seemingly irrelevant to its uniquely literary dimension, and the insurmountable relativism of language, its historical and social situatedness, referred to above: For the most part a mere testifier, the narrator is suspended in the observation of "scene," a succession of images minutely interwoven according not to any discernible logic of cause and effect, but to the formalist rule of aesthetics that says, "If it works, use it; if it doesn't, don't." And yet, as a member of the group, the narrator sets from within the narration the tone of disillusionment and skepticism to which the meaningless pretext for such a visit would indeed give rise. Though all overt expression of affect has been discarded with the anecdotal (and so too direct discourse, yet another mutation in Simonian narrative function), the reader senses the profound deception of one who has renounced the revolutionary illusion and the socialist myth. And herein lies Simon's extraordinary talent, for both this deception and the absurdity of any belief in a possible impact of the group's visit on the more precarious than ever world situation are powerfully rendered in *The Invitation* despite the complete absence of any novelistic rendering of either personal commentary or objective evaluation.

If the "pleasure" of this work derives from the openness of its signifying linguistic structures, on the one hand, and from the suspension of those narrative elements from which the reader expects to "profit," on the other, it comes as well from the often savage irony that is perhaps the only real unifying force in *The Invitation*. The historical situation, in all its banality, is in itself fundamentally ironic: Of the fifteen guests invited to the Soviet Union to act, through political and cultural dialogue, on the world order, all are celebrities of one sort or another and not one is a woman (even the female interpreters relinquish their posts to male counterparts when the secretary-general delivers his speech)—an odd sort of selectivism that makes a mockery of the attempt to harmonize the modern world. And the incongruous social and cultural makeup of the group is such that both the possibility of and reasons for any significant interaction between the visitors is thwarted. There to effect some degree of unanimity in the third millennium, they have but a limited means of communication (translation)--their languages serve more as obstacles than as means of mediation—and their disparities are divisive. Irony is further endemic to the situation insofar as it serves as a humoristic defense against the absurdity of excess: "Nero, dressed by the tailors of Savile Row, maintained that if they spoke so much it was to justify the expenditure made—for, divided by the greatest number of words possible, the price of each one of them would be established at a level acceptable to their accounting department" (37-38).

Simon is also ironic in his distancing of the crude historical reality of violence. As Colette Gaudin has remarked,

The violence of History is distanced by way of simple possibility ("the man who with a word could unleash an apocalypse") or it is connoted mythically in the surnames of Nero or Genghis Khan attributed to the personages. It is evoked in the immediate past of the regime, with the story "of the bandit with the iron name" and his successors, but it is not at the forefront of the narration.[2]

And he is ironic in his juxtaposing of freedom of form (the unconventional, ambiguous syntax or agrammatical use of language) with ritual (governmental protocol) and the imagistic allusion to repression. It must also be noted that *The Invitation* is a narrative of interminable speeches *never pronounced for the reader,* the narrative of endless dialogues *never spoken before the reader,* the narrative of tête-à-têtes *never verbalized within the text* (this by virtue of the descriptive mode privileged by the author) and that, as such, it is *within the ironic function of an unarticulated discourse that the fragmented semantics and fragmented syntax of the discourse that narrates it are unified.*

More subtle, however, but no less significant—and the source of the greatest "pleasure" of this text—is the irony of Simon's subversiveness: Inviting us into the Soviet Union, the author simultaneously turns us away. His writing pays witness not to the external environs, but to the internal impressions and fantasies they solicit, to a dynamism whose expression is unveiled, in the irony that is ultimately the measure of all art, as the metaphorical reflection of its own aesthetic production.

This is to say that, above all linguistic and narrative, cultural and political, and thematic and stylistic considerations, *The*

Afterword

Invitation's success lies in its positing not of the official visit that enframes the fiction, but of the existential suspension that is the invitational experience. Beyond any real delimitation of space or place (the strangeness of being outside one's own milieu, beyond the familiar, permeates the text from start to finish), beyond any real delimitation of time (the waiting for departures, as at the beginning and end of meetings and receptions, provides the only temporal marker), the narrative unfolds to reveal *the state of being elsewhere.* An *hors-lieu,* an *hors-temps,* the invitation is not so much Simon's to a foreign land as it is the reader's to participate in the revitalization of the fiction that each reading implies. It is in the perspective of the journey of interpretation and the production of meaning, therefore, that *The Invitation,* above all else, is a startling metaphor of its own creative constitution.

LOIS OPPENHEIM

NOTES

1   Claude Simon in *Three Decades of the French New Novel,* ed. Lois Oppenheim, trans. Lois Oppenheim and Evelyne Costa de Beauregard (Urbana: Univ. of Illinois Press, 1986), 74.
2   Colette Gaudin, "*L'Invitation:* les tentations de (Saint) Claude Simon" in *Revue des Sciences Humaines,* no. 220 (1990-4): 110 (my translation).

DALKEY ARCHIVE PAPERBACKS

FICTION

BARNES, DJUNA. *Ladies Almanack*	9.95
BARNES, DJUNA. *Ryder*	9.95
CHARTERIS, HUGO. *The Tide Is Right*	9.95
CRAWFORD, STANLEY. *Some Instructions to My Wife*	7.95
CUSACK, RALPH. *Cadenza*	7.95
DOWELL, COLEMAN. *Too Much Flesh and Jabez*	8.00
ERNAUX, ANNIE. *Cleaned Out*	9.95
FIRBANK, RONALD. *Complete Short Stories*	9.95
GASS, WILLIAM H. *Willie Masters' Lonesome Wife*	7.95
GRAINVILLE, PATRICK. *The Cave of Heaven*	9.95
MacLOCHLAINN, ALF. *Out of Focus*	5.95
MARKSON, DAVID. *Springer's Progress*	9.95
MARKSON, DAVID. *Wittgenstein's Mistress*	9.95
MOSLEY, NICHOLAS. *Accident*	7.95
MOSLEY, NICHOLAS. *Impossible Object*	7.95
MOSLEY, NICHOLAS. *Judith*	9.95
QUENEAU, RAYMOND. *The Last Days*	9.95
QUENEAU, RAYMOND. *Pierrot Mon Ami*	7.95
ROUBAUD, JACQUES. *The Great Fire of London*	12.95
SEESE, JUNE AKERS. *What Waiting Really Means*	7.95
SORRENTINO, GILBERT. *Imaginative Qualities of Actual Things*	9.95
SORRENTINO, GILBERT. *Splendide-Hôtel*	5.95
STEPHENS, MICHAEL. *Season at Coole*	7.95
TUSQUETS, ESTHER. *Stranded*	9.95
VALENZUELA, LUISA. *He Who Searches*	8.00
WOOLF, DOUGLAS. *Wall to Wall*	7.95
ZUKOFSKY, LOUIS. *Collected Fiction*	9.95

NONFICTION

GAZARIAN GAUTIER, MARIE-LISE. *Interviews with Spanish Writers*	14.95
MATHEWS, HARRY. *20 Lines a Day*	8.95
ROUDIEZ, LEON S. *French Fiction Revisited*	14.95
SHKLOVSKY, VIKTOR. *Theory of Prose*	12.95

POETRY

ANSEN, ALAN. *Contact Highs: Selected Poems*	11.95
FAIRBANKS, LAUREN. *Muzzle Thyself*	9.95